Bedtime With Blippi

This book belongs to:

www.Blippi.com

Written by Blippi Illustrated by Donald Guia

P9-DYX-838

It's bedtime for Blippi, the time when he dreams.

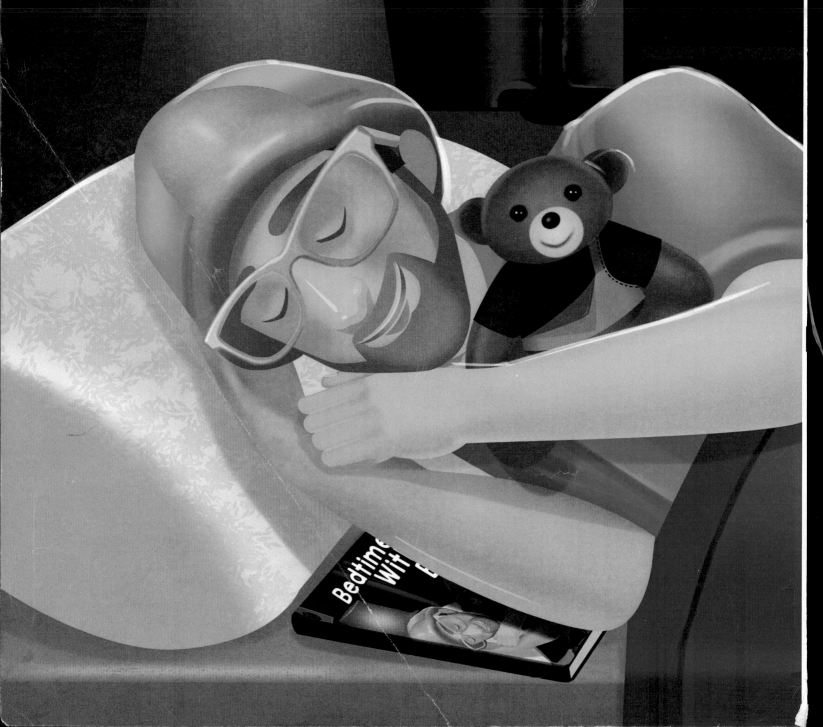

When he dreams things sometimes the dreams aren't what they seem.

Let's see what Blippi dreams!

Far from the ground
up in the blue sky,
Blippi flies the airplane
super duper high!

Deep in the water
so many kinds of creatures,
Blippi in the submarine
enjoys all of their features!

Floating in outer space heading to the moon, Blippi and the space ship will arrive there soon!

Lifting garbage into the back
BOOM SMASH CRUNCH CRASH!
Blippi with the garbage truck
takes out all of the trash!

Super loud sirens
flashing bright lights,
Blippi drives the police car
we're safe all day and night!

Floating on the water
with a rocking motion,
Blippi on the boat
in the bright blue ocean!

Jumping over cars
cheering from the crowd,
Blippi drives a monster truck
and revs the engine LOUD!

Early in the morning driving past the barn, Blippi in the tractor working on the farm!

Made in the USA
Lexington, KY
03 September 2018